Unplugged

Ella Gets Her Family Back

Laura Pedersen

Illustrated by Penny Weber

Tilbury House, Publishers · Gardiner, Maine

Ella

raced downstairs. She was excited about having blueberry waffles for breakfast because it was Friday—and because she'd thought of the perfect word (jinx) to use playing Hangman against her brother Carlos!

Her father sat at his computer in the living room reading the news. "Good morning, Daddy," said Ella.

Without turning around, he said, "Hi, Honey."

Carlos was already at the table playing a video game.

"Good morning, Carlos," said Ella. But he didn't seem to hear her. She quickly drew the hangman's scaffold and put four blank spaces below it, but Carlos ignored her.

Ella's mother had her briefcase in one hand and her cell phone in the other. She nodded toward the milk and cereal box already on the table.

"But you said we could have blueberry waffles as a treat today," Ella reminded her mother.

"Hold on," Ella's mother said into the phone. "I'm sorry, Ella, but I forgot. We'll have them tomorrow morning."

Ella's older sister Maya walked past the table and toward the door reading text messages on her cell phone.

"Wait!" said Ella. "You promised to do my hair before school."
Maya knew how to make all sorts of beautiful braids, even
inside-out ones.

"Tomorrow," said Maya as she walked out the door. "I have to
meet some friends now."

Ella scowled. Her family used to have breakfast together every morning and talk and laugh and play guessing games. Now all they did was stare at their screens and use their phones.

"Why can't we all talk together the way we used to?" she asked. But everyone was busy and no one answered.

That afternoon Ella rushed home from school and looked for her father, who had promised to go bike riding with her. But no one was home yet.

Suddenly Ella had an idea.

She went through the house collecting the charger cords for their phones and laptop computers, along with any small electronic devices she could find. In place of the things Ella took, she left notes that said, "Talk to Ella."

A moment after Ella finished, her mother arrived home and went to plug in her phone. "Ella, have you seen my charger? I left it right here on the counter."

"In here." Ella held up a laundry basket filled with cords and gadgets.

Maya came home from school and after a few minutes asked, "What have you done with my iPod?"

"In here." Ella pointed to the laundry basket.

Then Carlos came in, and when he saw the laundry basket, he said, "Give me back my stuff!"

"What's going on?" asked Ella's father, coming in the door.

"C'mon Ella," said Maya impatiently. "My phone battery is dead and my friends are trying to tell me where to meet them."

"And Ryan is on his way over to play video games with me!" said Carlos.

"I wish that nobody in this family had phones or video games or computers!" shouted Ella.

Ella's mother sat down and asked, "Is this your way of telling us that you think you're old enough to have a cell phone, too?"

"Do you feel left out because you're the only one in this family without a phone?" asked her father.

"No." Ella said. "I don't want a phone yet. I just want my family back. I want things to be like they were before you all got so plugged in."

She returned everyone's games and music players and phone chargers.
Her father plugged in his laptop and her sister ran off with her iPod
and phone charger and Carlos went to his room with his video game.

When Ella came downstairs the next morning, the rest of the family was sitting at the table and no one was texting or playing games or talking on the phone! Everyone was actually smiling at her.

Her father said, "Ella, we're making some changes. Breakfast is family time from now on."

A big smile crossed Ella's face. They did want to talk to her after all!

Her mother served them
all blueberry waffles.
"Eat up," said her father.
"You'll need your energy."

"We're all going for a bike ride today," said her mother.

"When?" asked Ella.

"Right after I beat you at Hangman," said her brother.

"Dream on!" said Ella. Because she already had a terrific word in mind—unplugged.

Tilbury House, Publishers
103 Brunswick Avenue
Gardiner, Maine 04345
800–582–1899 • www.tilburyhouse.com

First hardcover edition: October 2012 • 10 9 8 7 6 5 4 3 2 1

For Erin Elizabeth Suszynski, a girl who had endless imagination. —LP
For my family, who, like Ella's, would benefit from unplugging. —PW

Library of Congress Cataloging-in-Publication Data
Pedersen, Laura.
Unplugged : Ella gets her family back / Laura Pedersen ; illustrated by Penny
Weber. — 1st hardcover ed.
      p. cm.
Summary: Upset that her family is so focused on the screens on their various
electronic devices that they no longer talk, laugh, and play games together,
Ella takes all of their chargers and small devices.
ISBN 978-0-88448-337-3 (hardcover : alk. paper)
[1. Family life—Fiction. 2. Electronics—Fiction.] I. Weber, Penny, ill. II. Title.
PZ7.P34236Unp 2012
[E]—dc23
                                      2012024397

Designed by Geraldine Millham, Westport, Massachusetts
Printed and bound by Sung In Printing Ltd., Dang Jung-Dong 242-2, GungPo-si,
Kyunggi-do, Korea; August 2012.